Debbi Socha

HOW MUCH LONGER?!
(Instead Of... "Are We There Yet?!")

Bumblebee Books
London

A CIP catalogue record for this title is
available from the British Library.

ISBN: 978-1-83934-066-6

Bumblebee Books is an imprint of Olympia Publishers.

First Published in 2021

Bumblebee Books
Tallis House
2 Tallis Street
London
EC4Y 0AB

Printed in Great Britain

www.olympiapublishers.com

Dedication

To my angels in heaven, Nana and Grandma. To my angel here on Earth, Mom, and to my Kindergarten students of 2019-2020 whom I love dearly, Blake, Owen, Emmitt, Kameron, Greyson, Evan, Zain, Zeke, Levi, Johnny, Cooper, Amelia, Jade, Alexis, Aubree, Samantha, Annabella, Arianna, and Autumn.

All of a sudden,
I couldn't go to school.

I asked Momma,
"How much longer before I
go back to school?"

She said, "I don't know."

"How much longer before I get to see my friends again?"

"I don't know," she said.

I sat on the front steps and watched my cat curve her body around my doggie's tennis ball.

I thought, that's what my teacher would call a small moment... something to write about.

I went back inside the house and asked Momma, "How much longer before I get to see Miss Breen?"

I loved my teacher's hugs.

"I don't know,"
replied Momma.

I heard someone on TV talk about Kenny Rogers dying.

"Did Kenny Rogers die of the virus?" I asked Momma.

She chuckled. "No," said Momma. "He died of old age, or what they call natural causes. He was an amazing country singer my grandma loved and who I listened to growing up."

Morning meeting 9:10	Math 9:30	Music and Movement 10:10	Reading 10:30	Lunch 11:30	Writin 12:15
	Science 1:00	Social Studies 1:30	Snack 2:00	Free Play 2:20	Compu 2:45

The next morning, there was a schedule hanging on our kitchen wall. It looked like the one in my classroom.

"What's that for?"
I asked Momma.

"It's important for you to
have a schedule while you
are not in school."

"How much longer
before I go back?"

"I don't know," said Momma.

She started crying.

I decided 'how much longer' was not a good question anymore.

She stopped crying.
"Eventually it will end,"
she said.

HOW MUCH LONGER IS EVENTUALLY?!!!!!!

About the Author

I am a Kindergarten teacher at Midlakes Elementary School in Clifton Springs, NY, USA. I wrote this story thinking about what is happening with the coronavirus and how much I miss my kindergarten students. The part about my cat is true, as well as the part about growing up listening to my grandma's music and her appreciation of Kenny Rogers. This story was originally written on my kitchen notepad, after creating the story in my head while trying to sleep. This is my first published children's book.

Made in the USA
Middletown, DE
20 June 2021